STORY OF A PIEBALD HORSE
SOUTH AMERICAN ROMANCES

W.H. HUDSON

British Library Cataloguing-in-Publication Data
A catalogue record for this book is available from the
British Library

William Henry Hudson

William Henry Hudson was born on 4 August 1841 in a borough of Quilmes (now Florecio Varela) in Greater Buenos Aires, Argentina. His parents, Daniel and Catherine Hudson, were American settlers of English and Irish origin. His father was a sheep farmer on a small farm in Argentina, but was sadly unsuccessful. He then turned to potato growing for a paltry existence and this led the family to near financial ruin.

Hudson spent his childhood exploring the local flora and fauna and observing the natural and human drama, on what was a lawless frontier at that time. At around fourteen or fifteen, Hudson became seriously ill with a bout of typhus, soon followed by rheumatic fever. These illnesses permanently affected his health and caused him to become more studious and contemplative. His parents obtained many books for him and his siblings to read and he occasionally had some formal education from a visiting school teacher. Charles Darwin's (1809-1882) *The Origin of Species* (1859), in particular, made a lasting impression on him.

Little is known about Hudson in the period following his parents' death. He became a wanderer, occasionally publishing his ornithological work in the *Proceedings of the Zoological Society*. He initially wrote in an English that was interlaced with Spanish idioms. He appears to have particularly loved Patagonia. Hudson immigrated to London, England in 1869, where he eventually became a British subject in 1900. In 1876 he married a much older woman and they lived precariously on the money earned from two boarding houses that she owned. She eventually inherited a house in Bayswater, London and the couple moved there.

Hudson produced a series of ornithological studies throughout his life, including *Argentine Ornithology* (1888-1899) and *British Birds* (1895). These books on ornithological studies attracted the attention of the statesman, Sir Edward Grey (1862-1933), who got Hudson a state pension in 1901. Hudson later achieved fame with his books on the English countryside, such as *Hampshire Day* (1903), *Afoot in England* (1909), and *A Shepherd's Life* (1910), which helped foster the back to nature movement of the 1920s and 1930s. His most famous fictional novel was *Green Mansions* (1904) which was an exotic romance about a traveller in the Guyana Jungle in Venezuela and his encounter with a mysterious forest girl who is half human and half bird. This romance and some of Hudson's other romances attracted the friendship of other fiction writers, such as Joseph Conrad (1857-

1924), Ford Madox Ford (1873-1939) and George Gissing (1857-1903). Hudson's most popular non-fiction novel was *Far Away and Long Ago* (1918) which recalls his childhood in Argentina. Some of his other titles include *Birds and Man* (1901), *A Little Lost Boy* (1905), *Tales of the Pampas* (1916), *Ralph Herne* (1923), and *Mary's Little Lamb* (1929).

Away from his literary work, Hudson was a founding member of the Royal Society for the Protection of Birds. Towards the end of his life he moved to Worthing, Sussex, England. He died on 18 August 1922 and is buried at Broadwater and Worthing Cemetery in Worthing where his epitaph refers to his love of birds and green places. Even after his death, Hudson had a huge legacy. In Argentina where he is known as Guillermo Enrique Hudson, his work is considered to belong to the national literature. Ernest Hemingway (1899-1961) also famously refers to Hudson's early book *The Purple Land* (1885) in his novel *The Sun Also Rises* (1926) and again to Hudson's *Far Away and Long Ago* in his posthumous novel, *The Garden of Eden* (1986). Hudson has also had two South American bird species named after him as well as a town in Berazategui Partidd and several other public places and institutions.

STORY OF A PIEBALD HORSE

THIS is all about a piebald. People there are like birds that come down in flocks, hop about chattering, gobble up their seed, then fly away, forgetting what they have swallowed. I love not to scatter grain for such as these. With you, friend, it is different. Others may laugh if they like at the old man of many stories, who puts all things into his copper memory. I can laugh, too, knowing that all things are ordered by destiny ; otherwise I might sit down and cry.

The things I have seen ! There was the piebald that died long ago ; I could take you to the very spot where his bones used to lie bleaching in the sun. There is a nettle growing on the spot. I saw it yesterday. What important things are these to remember and talk about ! Bones of a dead horse and a nettle ; a young bird that falls from its nest in the night and is found dead in the morning : puffballs blown about by the wind : a little lamb left behind by the flock bleating at night amongst the thorns and thistles, where only the fox or wild dog can hear it ! Small matters are these, and our lives, what are they ? And the people we have known, the men and women who have spoken to us and touched us with warm hands—the bright eyes and red lips ! Can we cast these things like dead leaves on the fire ? Can we lie down full of heaviness because of them, and sleep and rise in the morning without them ? Ah, friend !

Let us to the story of the piebald. There was a cattle-marking at neighbour Sotelo's estancia, and out of a herd of three thousand head we had to part all the yearlings to be branded. After that, dinner and a dance. At sunrise we gathered, about thirty of us, all friends and neighbours, to do the work. Only with us came one person nobody knew. He joined us when we were on our way to the cattle ; a young man, slender, well-formed, of pleasing countenance and dressed as few could dress in those days. His horse also shone with silver trappings. And what an animal ! Many horses have I seen in this life, but never one with such a presence as this young stranger's piebald.

Arrived at the herd, we began to separate the young animals, the men riding in couples through the cattle, so that each calf when singled out could be driven by two horsemen, one on each side, to prevent it from doubling back. I happened to be mounted on a demon with a fiery mouth—there was no making him work, so I had to leave the parters and stand with little to do, watching the yearlings already parted, to keep them from returning to the herd.

Presently neighbour Chapaco rode up to me. He was a good-hearted man, well-spoken, half Indian and half Christian ; but he also had another half, and that was devil.

" What ! neighbour Lucero, are you riding on a donkey or a goat, that you remain here doing boy's work ? "

STORY OF A PIEBALD HORSE

I began telling him about my horse, but he did not listen ; he was looking at the parters.

" Who is that young stranger ? " he asked.

" I see him to-day," I replied, " and if I see him again to-morrow then I shall have seen him twice."

" And in what country of which I have never heard did he learn cattle-parting ? " said he.

" He rides," I answered, " like one presuming on a good horse. But he is safe, his fellow-worker has all the danger."

" I believe you," said Chapaco. " He charges furiously and hurls the heifer before his comrade, who has all the work to keep it from doubling, and all the danger, for at any moment his horse may go over it and fall. This our young stranger does knowingly, thinking that no one here will resent it. No, Lucero, he is presuming more on his long knife than on his good horse."

Even while we spoke, the two we were watching rode up to us. Chapaco saluted the young man, taking off his hat, and said—" Will you take me for a partner, friend? "

" Yes ; why not, friend ? " returned the other ; and together the two rode back to the herd.

Now I shall watch them, said I to myself, to see what this Indian devil intends doing. Soon they came out of the herd driving a very small animal. Then I knew what was coming. " May your guardian angel be with you to avert a calamity, young stranger ! " I exclaimed. Whip and spur those two came towards me like men riding a race and not parting cattle. Chapaco kept close to the calf, so that he had the advantage, for his horse was well trained. At length he got a little ahead, then, quick as lightning, he forced the calf round square before the other. The piebald struck it full in the middle, and fell because it had to fall. But, Saints in Heaven! why did not the rider save himself? Those who were watching saw him throw up his feet to tread his horse's neck and leap away; nevertheless man, horse, and calf, came down together. They ploughed the ground for some distance so great had been their speed, and the man was under. When we picked him up he was senseless, the blood flowing from his mouth. Next morning, when the sun rose and God's light fell on the earth, he expired.

Of course there was no dancing that night. Some of the people, after eating, went away; others remained sitting about all night, talking in low tones, waiting for the end. A few of us were at his bedside watching his white face and closed eyes. He breathed, and that was all. When the sunlight came over the world he opened his eyes, and Sotelo asked him how he did. He took no notice, but presently his lips began to move, though they seemed to utter no sound. Sotelo bent his ear down to listen. "Where does she live?" he asked. He could not answer—he was dead.

"He seemed to be saying many things," Sotelo told us, "but I understood only this—'Tell her to forgive me . . . I was wrong. She loved him from the first . . . I was jealous, and hated him. . . . Tell Elaria not to grieve—Anacleto will be good to her.' Alas! my friends, where shall I find his relations to deliver this dying message to them?"

STORY OF A PIEBALD HORSE

The Alcalde came that day and made a list of the dead man's possessions, and bade Sotelo take charge of them till the relations could be found. Then, calling all the people together, he bade each person cut on his whip-handle and on the sheath of his knife the mark branded on the flank of the piebald, which was in shape like a horse-shoe with a cross inside, so that it might be shown to all strangers, and made known through the country until the dead man's relations should hear of it.

When a year had gone by, the Alcalde told Sotelo that, all inquiries having failed, he could now take the piebald and the silver trappings for himself. Sotelo would not listen to this, for he was a devout man and coveted no person's property, dead or alive. The horse and things, however, still remained in his charge.

Three years later I was one afternoon sitting with Sotelo, taking maté, when his herd of dun mares were driven up. They came galloping and neighing to the corral and ahead of them, looking like a wild horse, was the piebald, for no person ever mounted him.

" Never do I look on that horse," I remarked, " without remembering the fatal marking, when its master met his death."

" Now you speak of it," said he, " let me inform you that I am about to try a new plan. That noble piebald and all those silver trappings hanging in my room are always reproaching my conscience. Let us not forget the young stranger we put under ground. I have had many masses said for his soul's repose, but that does not quite satisfy me. Somewhere there is a place where he is not forgotten. Hands there are, perhaps, that gather wild flowers to place them with lighted candles before the image of the Blessed Virgin ; eyes there are that weep and watch for his coming. You know how many travellers and cattle-drovers going to Buenos Ayres from the south call for refreshment at the *pulperia*. I intend taking the piebald and tying him every day at the gate there. No person calling will fail to notice the horse, and some day perhaps some traveller will recognise the brand on its flank and will be able to tell us what department and what estancia it comes from."

1 did not believe anything would result from this, but said nothing, not wishing to discourage him.

Next morning the piebald was tied up at the gate of the *pulperia*, at the road side, only to be released again when night came, and this was repeated every day for a long time. So fine an animal did not fail to attract the attention of all strangers passing that way, still several weeks went by and nothing was discovered. At length, one evening, just when the sun was setting, there appeared a troop of cattle driven by eight men. It had come a great distance, for the troop was a large one—about nine hundred head—and they moved slowly, like cattle that had been many days on the road. Some of the men came in for refreshments ; then the store-keeper noticed that one remained outside leaning on the gate.

" What is the capatas doing that he remains outside ? " said one of the men.

" Evidently he has fallen in love with that piebald," said another, " for he cannot take his eyes off it."

STORY OF A PIEBALD HORSE

At length the capatas, a young man of good presence, came in and sat down on a bench. The others were talking and laughing about the strange things they had all been doing the day before; for they had been many days and nights on the road, only nodding a little in their saddles, and at length becoming delirious from want of sleep, they had begun to act like men that are half-crazed.

" Enough of the delusions of yesterday," said the capatas, who had been silently listening to them, " but tell me, boys, am I in the same condition to-day ? "

" Surely not ! " they replied. " Thanks to those horned devils being so tired and footsore, we all had some sleep last night."

" Very well then," said he, " now you have finished eating and drinking, go back to the troop, but before you leave look well at that piebald tied at the gate. He that is not a cattle-drover may ask, ' How can my eyes deceive me ? ' but I know that a crazy brain makes us see many strange things when the drowsy eyes can only be held open with the fingers."

The men did as they were told, and when they had looked well at the piebald, they all shouted out, " He has the brand of the estancia de Silva on his flank, and no counter-brand—claim the horse, capatas, for he is yours." And after that they rode away to the herd.

" My friend," said the capatas to the store-keeper, " will you explain how you came possessed of this piebald horse ? "

Then the other told him everything, even the dying words of the young stranger, for he knew all.

STORY OF A PIEBALD HORSE

The capatas bent down his head, and covering his face shed tears. Then he said, " And you died thus, Torcuato, amongst strangers ! From my heart I have forgiven you the wrong you did me. Heaven rest your soul, Torcuato ; I cannot forget that we were once brothers. ' I, friend, am that Anacleto of whom he spoke with his last breath."

Sotelo was then sent for, and when he arrived and the *pulperia* was closed for the night, the capatas told his story, which I will give you in his own words, for I was also present to hear him. This is what he told us :—

I was born on the southern frontier. My parents died when I was very small, but Heaven had compassion on me and raised up one to shelter me in my orphanhood. Don Loreto Silva took me to his estancia on the Sarandi, a stream half a day's journey from Tandil, towards the setting sun. He treated me like one of his own children, and I took the name of Silva. He had two other children, Torcuato, who was about the same age as myself, and his daughter, Elaria, who was younger. He was a widower when he took charge of me, and died when I was still a youth. After his death we moved to Tandil, where we had a house close to the little town ; for we were all minors, and the property had been left to be equally divided between us when we should be of age. For four years we lived happily together ; ,then when we were of age we preferred to keep the property undivided. I proposed that we should go and live on the estancia, but Torcuato would not consent, liking the place where we were living best. Finally, not being able to persuade him, I resolved to go and attend to the estancia myself. He said that I could please myself and that he should stay where he was with Elaria. It was only when I told Elaria of these things that I knew how much I loved her. She wept and implored me not to leave her.

"Why do you shed tears, Elaria?" I said; "is it because you love me? Know, then, that I also love you with all my heart, and if you will be mine, nothing can ever make us unhappy. Do not think that my absence at the estancia will deprive me of this feeling which has ever been growing up in me."

"I do love you, Anacleto," she replied, "and I have also known of your love for a long time. But there is something in my heart which I cannot impart to you; only I ask you, for the love you bear me, do not leave me, and do not ask me why I say this to you."

After this appeal I could not leave her, nor did I ask her to tell me her secret. Torcuato and I were friendly, but not as we had been before this difference. I had no evil thoughts of him; I loved him and was with him continually; but from the moment I announced to him that I had changed my mind about going to the estancia, and was silent when he demanded the reason, there was a something in him which made it different between us. I could not open my heart to him about Elaria, and sometimes I thought that he also had a secret which he had no intention of sharing with me. This coldness did not, however, distress me very much, so great was the happiness I now experienced, knowing that I possessed Elaria's love. He was much away from the house, being fond of amusements, and he had also begun to gamble. About three months passed in this way, when one morning Torcuato, who was saddling his horse to go out, said, " Will you come with me, to-day, Anacleto ? "

" I do not care to go," I answered.

" Look, Anacleto," said he ; " once you were always ready to accompany me to a race or dance, or cattle-marking. Why have you ceased to care for these things ? Are you growing devout before your time, or does my company no longer please you ? "

" It is best to tell him everything and have done with secrets," said I to myself, and so replied—

" Since you ask me, Torcuato, I will answer you frankly. It is true that I now take less pleasure than formerly in these pastimes ; but you have not guessed the reason rightly."

" What then is this reason of which you speak ? "

" Since you cannot guess it," I replied, " know that it is love."

" Love for whom ? " he asked quickly, and turning very pale.

" Do you need ask ? Elaria," I replied.

I had scarcely uttered the name before he turned on me full of rage.

" Elaria ! " he exclaimed. " Do you dare tell me of love for Elaria ! But you are only a blind fool, and do not know that I am going to marry her myself."

" Are you mad, Torcuato, to talk of marrying your sister ? "

" She is no more my sister than you are my brother," he

returned. " I," he continued, striking his breast passionately, " am the only child of my father, Loreto Silva. Elaria, whose mother died in giving her birth, was adopted by my parents. And because she is going to be my wife, I am willing that she should have a share of the property ; but you, a miserable foundling, why were you lifted up so high ? Was it not enough that you were clothed and fed till you came to man's estate ? Not a hand's-breadth of the estancia land should be yours by right, and now you presume to speak of love for Elaria."

My blood was on fire with so many insults, but I remembered all the benefits I had received from his father, and did not raise my hand against him. Without more words he left me. I then hastened to Elaria and told her what had passed.

" This," I said, " is the secret you would not impart to me. Why, when you knew these things, was I kept in ignorance ? "

" Have pity on me, Anacleto," she replied, crying. " Did I not see that you two were no longer friends and brothers, and this without knowing of each other's love ? I dared not open my lips to you or to him. It is always a woman's part to suffer in silence. God intended us to be poor, Anacleto, for we were both born of poor parents, and had this property never come to us, how happy we might have been ! "

" Why do you say such things, Elaria ? Since we love each other, we cannot be unhappy, rich or poor."

" Is it a little matter," she replied, " that Torcuato must be our bitter enemy ? But you do not know everything.

STORY OF A PIEBALD HORSE

Before Torcuato's father died, he said he wished his son to marry me when we came of age. When he spoke about it we were sitting together by his bed."

" And what did you say, Elaria ? " I asked, full of concern.

" Torcuato promised to marry me. I only covered my face, and was silent, for I loved you best even then, though I was almost a child, and my heart was filled with grief at his words. After we came here, Torcuato reminded me of his father's words. I answered that I did not wish to marry him, that he was only a brother to me. Then he said that we were young and he could wait until I was of another mind. This is all I have to say ; but how shall we three live together any longer ? I cannot bear to part from you, and every moment I tremble to think what may happen when you two are together."

" Fear nothing," I said. " To-morrow morning you can go to spend a week at some friend's house in the town ; then I will speak to Torcuato, and tell him that since we cannot live in peace together we must separate. Even if he answers with insults I shall do nothing to grieve you, and if he refuses to listen to me, I shall send some person we both respect to arrange all things between us."

This satisfied her, but as evening approached she grew paler, and I knew she feared Torcuato's return. He did not, however, come back that night. Early next morning she was ready to leave. It was an easy walk to the town-but the dew was heavy on the grass, and I saddled a horse for her to ride. I had just lifted her to the saddle when Torcuato appeared. He came at great speed, and throwing himself off his horse, advanced to us. Elaria trembled and seemed ready to sink upon the earth to hide herself like a partridge that has seen the hawk. I prepared myself for insults and perhaps violence. He never looked at me; he only spoke to her.

"Elaria," he said, "something has happened—something that obliges me to leave this house and neighbourhood at once. Remember when I am away that my father, who cherished you and enriched you with his bounty, and who also cherished and enriched this ingrate, spoke to us from his dying bed and made me promise to marry you, Think what his love was; do not forget that his last wish is sacred, and that Anacleto has acted a base, treacherous part in trying to steal you from me. He was lifted out of the mire to be my brother and equal in everything except this. He has got a third part of my inheritance—let that satisfy him; your own heart, Elaria, will tell you that a marriage with him would be a crime before God and man. Look not for my return to-morrow nor for many days. But if you two begin to laugh at my father's dying wishes, look for me, for then I shall not delay to come back to you, Elaria, and to you, Anacleto. I have spoken."

He then mounted his horse and rode away. Very soon we learned the cause of his sudden departure. He had quarrelled over his cards and in a struggle that followed had stabbed his adversary to the heart. He had fled to escape the penalty. We did not believe that he would remain long absent; for Torcuato was very young, well off, and much liked, and this was, moreover, his first offence against the law. But time went on and he did not return, nor did any message from him reach us, and we at last concluded that he had left the country. Only now, after four years, have I accidentally discovered his fate through seeing his piebald horse.

After he had been absent over a year, I asked Elaria to become my wife. " We cannot marry till Torcuato returns," she said. " For if we take the property that ought to have been all his, and at the same time disobey his father's dying wish, we shall be doing an evil thing. Let us take care of the property till he returns to receive it all back from us ; then, Anacleto, we shall be free to marry."

I consented, for she was more to me than lands and cattle. I put the estancia in order, and leaving a trustworthy person in charge of everything I invested my money in fat bullocks to resell in Buenos Ayres, and in this business I have been employed ever since. From the estancia I have taken nothing, and now it must all come back to us—his inheritance and ours. This is a bitter thing and will give Elaria great grief.

Thus ended Anacleto's story, and when he had finished speaking and still seemed greatly troubled in his mind, Sotelo said to him, " Friend, let me advise you what to do. You will now shortly be married to the woman you love and probably some day a son will be born to you. Let him be named Torcuato, and let Torcuato's inheritance be kept for him. And if God gives you no son, remember what was done for you and for the girl you are going to marry, when you were orphans and friendless, and look out for some unhappy child in the same condition, to protect and enrich him as you were enriched."

"You have spoken well," said Anacleto. "I will report your words to Elaria, and whatever she wishes done that will I do."

So ends my story, friend. The cattle-drover left us that night and we saw no more of him. Only before going he gave the piebald and the silver trappings to Sotelo. Six months after his visit, Sotelo also received a letter from him to say that his marriage with Elaria had taken place ; and the letter was accompanied with a present of seven cream-coloured horses with black manes and hoofs.